THE
ELEPHANT
IN THE
BARN

the ELEPHANT

THE

ELEPHANT

IN THE

BARN

by JAMES PLAYSTED WOOD

Pictures by LEONARD KESSLER

HARPER & ROW, PUBLISHERS, NEW YORK AND EVANSTON

for BET

THE
ELEPHANT
IN THE
BARN

1

Stephen, who was nine, lived with his mother and father and Susan, who was six, and David, who was four, in a wonderful old house beside a deep dingle, or wooded hollow, with more high woods and a shining river behind the house.

Stephen was having a happy time in school. His class was having nature study, and each day the teacher let one of the class bring a pet to school.

One day one of the boys brought his white rabbit in a wire-covered box. The rabbit blinked his pink eyes at the children, and they fed him crisp lettuce leaves and watched him all day. Another day one of the girls brought a pair of brightly colored parakeets, and they watched them flit back and forth on their perches and listened to them talk to each other. Then a boy brought his soft little guinea pig, and one of the other children brought a tiny white mouse, and another one brought a beautiful fantail pigeon that spread its tail and stalked back and forth like a little white peacock.

"Tomorrow," asked Stephen, "may I bring our elephant?"

"Of course," said the teacher. "Elephants are very interesting, and we'd all love to see your elephant."

She acted as if she did not think that Stephen and Susan and David really had an elephant at all.

They did, though. Early one warm morning in the spring Stephen had gone out to their big red barn to pump up a tire on his bicycle, and there the elephant was. He had swum across the river the night before and gone into the barn to sleep. Susan and Stephen and David, and even mother and father and Jones, their spaniel, and the kittens, Topsy and Turvy, were all so pleased that the elephant had stayed with the family ever since, and he said he was never going away.

All the golden summer long the elephant had played with Susan, Stephen, and David. They had gone on picnics and swimming in the river and camping. They had had parties on the lawn and in the barn, and on rainy days the elephant had told them stories. The elephant claimed they were true, but sometimes he seemed to be making them up, and they got bigger and bigger as he went along.

That afternoon after school Stephen, excited, though he was usually very quiet, told the ele-

phant that they would be going to school together the next morning.

"Oh, I don't know," said the elephant, shaking his head a little. "I don't know at all. It's a
long time since I went to school."

"But you know all about it," said Susan
quickly. "You said you did."

"Of course, I do," said the elephant, who
never admitted that he did not know all about
everything, "but I don't feel very well."

"Next year *I'm* going to school!" cried David.

"You're not a bit sick, and you know it!"
Susan scolded the elephant.

"All right!" said the elephant suddenly. "I'll
go. I want to see that teacher about Stephen's
arithmetic paper she said was wrong."

"It *was* wrong," said Stephen. "Teacher said
it was. She said the answer was much too big."

The elephant had been helping Stephen with
his homework.

"It wasn't too big for me," explained the elephant. "Elephants have to have bigger numbers than people." He thought if they got talking about something else they might forget about making him go to school, but Susan saw the look in his eye.

"That doesn't matter now," she said. "We have to get you all cleaned up for school tomorrow. Let's get our bathing suits, and we'll give you a good bath."

"But I've had a bath!" complained the elephant. He really didn't mind, but he always objected to everything the first time anyway.

So Susan and Stephen and David hurried into their bathing suits. They got out the garden hose and attached it. They brought out stepladders, and Susan got soap, brushes, and a whole big box of washing powder. The elephant stood still in the center of the side lawn. He was thinking hard, and he thought he had a plan which would save him from going to school.

Stephen climbed to the top of the stepladder on one side of the elephant with a pail and a scrubbing brush and a big cake of yellow soap.

"Now!" he called, and Susan turned the hose right on the elephant, who closed his eyes tight.

Stephen scrubbed away at the elephant's side and back, and David, who had a smaller brush and another cake of soap, scrubbed away at one of the elephant's front feet. Susan kept pouring on more water.

"Stop wriggling!" cried Stephen, who was wet and covered with lather.

"I can't help it!" said the elephant. "It tickles!" He kept his eyes closed so as not to get any soap in them and tried to be still. Inside, he had begun laughing to himself.

"You're getting all shiny and beautiful!" cried Susan. "You'll be the prettiest pupil in the school!"

"Oh, no, I won't," said the elephant to himself. He smiled a little, but it was hard because
some of the soap had dried on his face, and it
cracked when he smiled.

David, who was working on another foot now,
let out a howl and began to cry.

"David! What is it?" asked Susan, alarmed.

David sitting under the elephant, had put
down his scrubbing brush. He was wet and drip-
ping from the water pouring off the elephant. He
put his face in his arms and cried some more.

"David! Did you hurt yourself?" Holding the
hose a different way so that the water would still
squirt on the elephant, Susan bent over David.

"I want to go to school!" sobbed David. "I
want to go to school! Everybody goes to school
except me."

"But you're going next year!"

"I want to go now!" sobbed David. "I want
to go *now*!"

Susan thought quickly of something to make

7

David feel better. She began to whisper to him. The elephant opened one eye because he thought he could hear better with one eye open, but he couldn't see them because they were underneath him.

"It's not polite to whisper," he said, just as if he never whispered himself.

David stopped crying, and he and Susan began to laugh.

"Stephen!" called Susan. "Help David up." She pushed David up the stepladder, and Stephen pulled him up the rest of the way.

In his hand David had the big box of soap powder which Susan had opened for him. He poured it over the elephant's back. Susan doused on more water, and suddenly the elephant was covered with big soap bubbles, shiny and full of rainbow colors.

David hurried back down, and Stephen came down too, and they looked at the elephant. He was covered with big bubbles, and some were sailing off him and bursting in the sunlight.

"The elephant's all bubbles! The elephant is a great big bubble! I made the biggest bubble in the world!" shouted David, jumping up and down on the lawn.

The elephant was so surprised he opened his eyes wide. Just as he opened them, a great big bubble burst right in front of his trunk.

"You've got soap in my eyes!" he cried. "I have soap in my eyes!"

He began to jump up and down because the soap stung his eyes. Thousands and thousands of bubbles flew into the air and sailed away. Some of them went to the top of the small trees on the lawn before they burst.

Stephen took a towel, climbed the ladder again, and wiped off the elephant's face, wiping very carefully around his eyes.

"Soap in my eyes!" cried the elephant. "It hurts!"

"It doesn't hurt *that* much!" scolded Susan.

"You are too big to make such a fuss. When I get soap in my eyes, I don't cry."

"It hurts more when you're bigger," said the elephant, winking and blinking and squinting. He let out an even louder cry as he thought of something else that might help his scheme. "I certainly won't be able to go to school now. I'd not be able to read with soap in my eyes."

"It will all be gone by then," said Stephen. He climbed right up into the bubbles, which half hid him, and began to wash the other side of the elephant.

"No it won't," said the elephant, peering around him as if he could not see. "It will be much worse. I can tell."

"Do stop wriggling," said Stephen. "I can't get you clean all over if you keep wriggling."

"I suppose you want me to stop breathing, too, so my sides won't go in and out!" complained the elephant bitterly.

10

"That would help," said Stephen calmly. "Oh!"

Susan was so busy washing the bubbles off the elephant that she had turned the hose full on Stephen and almost washed him off the elephant too.

"See," said the elephant, as Stephen dropped his brush and pail to hang onto him. "That shows I was right."

"It just shows I made a mistake and shot Stephen with the water instead of you," said Susan. "Oh, you're getting clean as clean. Even Mother will be satisfied."

"I want to turn the elephant into a big bubble again!" cried David, dancing up and down on the grass. "Let me turn him into a million bubbles again!"

"Whatever you do," said the elephant sadly, "I won't be able to go to school tomorrow."

He looked at Susan and Stephen out of the

corner of his eye to see what they would say to that. As Susan was on one side of him with the hose and Stephen was on top of him, he looked funny trying to see them both at once.

"Why can't you go to school?" they both demanded.

"Because I'm too wet," said the elephant happily. "I won't be dry in time."

"You'll be dry in a half hour," said Susan.

"Certainly you will," said Stephen. "We have ten old kitchen towels and an old rug off the back porch Mother said we could dry you with. Then you can stand in the sun."

Susan had turned off the hose now that all the soap and lather had been washed off the elephant. David was wading through some of the puddles the water had made on the lawn. One big bubble, which had not yet burst but was a little lopsided, seemed to be looking at them from a high branch on the old cherry tree. It looked almost like the man in the moon who had made a mistake and come out before dark.

The elephant shook his head more sadly than before. "I really wanted to go to school very much," he said, just as if he meant it, "but now I'm too wet."

"You're already getting dry. Look!" said Susan, who was rubbing one of the elephant's knees with a towel.

"Oh, that!" said the elephant, looking at the place. "That doesn't count. That's just on the outside. You put so much water on me that I'm all wet *inside*!"

"You couldn't be!" exclaimed Stephen, who had never thought of that. He was not sure, though.

"It soaked right through me," explained the elephant. "Look!" He blew out pails full of water he had been saving up his trunk. It made a bigger fountain than even Susan's hose had

done and splashed down all over a big bush.

"Are you really wet inside?" asked Susan anxiously. "Oh, I wish I had not squirted so much water on you!"

"It will take days for me to dry out," said the

14

elephant. "I don't know how many days. Listen!" He gurgled as if he were full of water. "I'll not be able to go to school at all."

"Good!" shouted David. "Now you can stay home with me. I don't go to school either."

"Yes," said the elephant, as if he were sorry he could not go to school. "I'll have to stay home with you, David." His scheme had worked. He didn't really want to go to school, and he was not sorry they thought he had to stay home. "Your mother or father will have to write me an excuse," he said, as if his heart were broken.

"An excuse?" asked Stephen.

"Of course! Just the way they have to do when you or Susan can't go to school."

"But you've never even been to school yet," said Stephen.

"That doesn't make any difference," said the elephant firmly. So that night the children's mother wrote a note. It said:

15

Dear Teacher:

    Please excuse the elephant for being
absent from school today. He is not
well.

Susan and Stephen showed it to the elephant
before they took it carefully to school the next
morning.

2

As Halloween came near, the elephant, who had never been out that night, was even more excited than Susan, Stephen, and David. The children's father had bought pumpkins for them all, and they had picked out the very biggest from the heap on the farmer's lawn for the elephant's jack-o'-lantern.

They had cut noses and mouths and eyes in the pumpkins in the barn, and now the elephant did not want to wait even one more day for Halloween. He wanted to light his lantern and go out into the night just as soon as it got dark.

"No," said Susan firmly. "We have to wait. You can't get all dressed up and do Trick or Treat until Halloween night itself."

"Yes, but we ought to practice," argued the elephant.

They could still see, but it was getting dark in the barn. The kittens, Topsy and Turvy, were playing in some old hay and straw. Suddenly Topsy raced across the floor and jumped right into the elephant's hollow pumpkin. The elephant snatched the kitten out and just as quickly tried to put the pumpkin over his head. It was far too small. "Boo!" he said to Topsy. "G-rrr!"

Topsy was not frightened a bit, but their spaniel, Jones, who was trying to climb down a tiny mouse hole in one corner of the barn, jumped back and began to bark furiously, as if the mouse had leaped out and tried to bite him.

Just then the big barn door slid back noiselessly a few inches as it was slowly opened from the outside. Suddenly two fiery staring eyes, a bright mouth, and a long fiery nose were blazing in at them.

"Oh!" gasped Susan.

The elephant, who had been sitting in the middle of the wide floor, jumped startled to his feet. Jones barked even more loudly, and the two kittens leaped with flashing claws for the rafters.

The staring face moved slowly into the barn. "Doesn't it look good?" asked Stephen, who had been holding a small flashlight inside his Halloween pumpkin.

"Oh!" breathed Susan.

"I thought—" said the elephant, his voice trembling a little, "I thought it was a—a something." Then to show that he had not been frightened at all he said, "What do people give you? Licorice drops? Candied ginger? I hope we get some ginger sandwiches."

"Apples," said David. "Mostly apples. And we don't need any old apples. We have lots of apples."

"Oh, lots of things," said Susan." Cookies and candy and—"

"And if they don't give us anything I just knock their houses down on top of them!" said the elephant happily.

"You don't do anything of the kind," said Stephen. "You only stand there and say, 'Trick or Treat,' and if they don't give you anything, you just go away."

David had put the elephant's big pumpkin head on. It was so big it came right down over his head and rested on his shoulders. "Whooo!" he said from inside, his voice muffled and scary. "Whooo!"

"Mother's getting our costumes all ready,"

21

said Susan excitedly. "I am going to be a witch out of the dingle, and Stephen is going to be a black cat, and David is going to be a mouse. The cat will chase the mouse, and the witch will chase them both."

"What am I going to be?" asked the elephant eagerly. "What costume is your mother making for me?"

It was really dark now. Stephen kept his pumpkin lighted, and it was all the light they had. It shone through the lantern's eyes and mouth and nose and made queer shadows everywhere inside the barn.

"Why—" said Susan. She did not know what to say. Their mother wasn't making any costume for the elephant. He was too big. She did not want to tell the elephant that because his feelings might be hurt. Then she thought of something. "You're going to be there to take care of us all after dark. That's what Mother said. Remember?"

It was so dark and strange inside the barn that they had begun to whisper.

"But what shall I be?" whispered the elephant. "I have to be something."

"I know," whispered Stephen. "You'll be an elephant."

"But I *am* an elephant."

"Of course, you are," said Susan quickly. "That will surprise them more than anything."

"You can wear my mouse suit," whispered David, who had taken off his extra head. "Then I'll be an elephant."

"That's silly," said Stephen. "We haven't any elephant costume for you."

"You should be yourself," Susan whispered to the elephant. "An elephant's the best thing anybody can be. You always say that."

"I know," said the elephant suddenly. "I'll wear a black mask. I can make one out of those old window shades. Nobody will know who I am then. Give the password."

"Trick or Treat," said Stephen, marching out.

"Trick or Treat," said David, following him.

Susan waited a minute. "Good-night," she said to the elephant. "Just one more day to wait. I'm going to wear a mask, too. Trick or Treat."

Halloween night, as soon as it was dark, they all crept out of their driveway and started down the quiet, wide old street of big old houses toward the town. There were lights on the porches or over the doorsteps, black shadows behind the big maples along the road. A golden shaving of moon was just slipping noiselessly up into the sky from behind the night-black woods which lay behind the houses toward the river.

"S-sssh!" warned the elephant, walking very quietly. He was carrying his big pumpkin head carefully so the flashlight would not fall out. He wore a huge black mask across his face with just his eyes looking out.

Stephen held David tightly by one hand, and Susan held him by the other. They all had their

24

pumpkins lighted, and they each carried a big bag to bring home their treasure. Susan's bag was already heavy and she carried it very care-fully, for she had something inside it that none of the others knew about.

"And the elephant's going to knock down their houses on top of them if we don't like what they give us!" cried David happily.

"No, he isn't," said Stephen, holding onto his big cat's whiskers so they would not get knocked off against one of the trees.

"Then I will!" said David.

"Scuff-scuff-scuff" went the elephant's feet along the dark sidewalk. A thin night breeze sifted through the leaves that were still on the trees. Little stars blinked down through the branches. The deep woods toward the river looked almost as if they might have real witches in them.

The houses were far apart on the old street where the edge of the city touched the woods

and hills. It was dark and still. Susan, holding tight to her bag and her broomstick and her pumpkin and David, shrank a little against the elephant. She was glad the elephant was with them. Stephen pretended to be very brave.

"I hope we get some pretzels," said David, picking up his mouse tail and stuffing the end into his pocket.

"Pretzels are all right," said the elephant, wondering if the bag he had brought was large enough, "and doughnuts are always good, but I hope we get some licorice drops. I like licorice drops the best."

"Me first!" cried David, as they came to the first house. He let go of the others' hands and ran up the steps. He rang the doorbell and knocked on the door and pounded the old brass knocker all at once.

"My goodness!" cried a white-haired old lady, who came quickly. "A witch and a cat and a mouse! Please don't hurt me, Mrs. Witch! Now let me see—I'm afraid I don't have any cheese for the mouse or fish for the cat. All I have is cookies and candy, and I don't suppose—"

"We'll take them!" cried David quickly. "I'm not a real mouse. I'm David."

"Thank you," said Susan and David, as they stuffed candies and cookies into their bags.

They ran back to the elephant, who had hidden behind a tree in the darkness to see how it was done.

"See!" said David, holding it up to him. "I got a shiny penny, too."

When they came to the next house, David raced again for the steps, but the elephant held him back. "My turn," he said. He knocked on the door, and they all waited. It was colder now and even quieter, though away off between the houses they could see jack-o'-lanterns bobbing on another street and hear people laughing.

A pretty young woman opened the door this time. "Madam," said the elephant, who forgot what he was supposed to say, "my friends and I —have you any licorice drops?"

The young woman just stared at him, her eyes growing larger and larger.

Stephen nudged the elephant. "Trick or Treat," he reminded him.

"Trick or Treat!" shouted the elephant, more loudly than he had intended. His mask had slipped over one eye so that he looked almost like a pirate.

The young woman did not even shut the door. She just turned and ran down the hall and up the stairs.

The elephant was very much annoyed. "I'll pull her house down," he said.

"No," said Susan quickly. "Mother said we were to be very polite."

The elephant, who did not have anything in his bag yet, was getting hungry. David had eaten everything out of his except the shiny penny.

"It's still my turn," the elephant insisted when they came to another big old house set back on wide lawns. "They had better give us some licorice drops."

It was a man who answered the door this time. He looked at the elephant a minute, and then he laughed. "I think it is a very good idea, young lady," he said to Susan, "for your father to come along to look after you." He called to his wife. "Myra, we have guests!"

A lady came with a big tray heaped with apples and oranges and figs and gingerbread. There was even a big china pot full of cocoa, and she poured out a steaming cupful for each of the children.

"I meant what I said," the man told the ele-

31

phant. "I think it is fine of you to come along with the children. More fathers should do that kind of thing."

"I'm not the father," said the elephant. "I'm an elephant."

The man laughed. "I forgot for a minute. At least we can have a cigar and a chat while they are drinking their cocoa. I think you'll like this cigar. Here, let me light it for you."

"I don't smoke," said the elephant.

"I know better than that," said the man. "I've never seen you without your pipe." He held a match to the cigar he had placed in the elephant's mouth.

The elephant coughed and spluttered as he and the smiling man smoked. He looked longingly at the cocoa that Susan, Stephen, and David were drinking. Then he couldn't see it because the smoke brought tears to his eyes.

After they had finished their cocoa, the lady

heaped their bags with candy and cake and fruit. The man slapped the elephant on the back and said again how glad he was the elephant had come with the children, and they went out into the night once more.

"Oh!" said the elephant, as soon as the door had closed behind them. "Oh! Oh! Oh!" He sat down on the curbstone between the sidewalk and the road under the big trees. "Oh!"

"What's the matter?" exclaimed Susan.

"I'm on fire! That's what the matter is," said the elephant. "Look!" He held out his trunk. Little wisps of smoke were curling out of its end. "I don't feel well, either." He lay down.

"You'll be all right, I think," said Stephen, though he wasn't sure. "Perhaps if you eat one of these apples you will feel better."

"You must go on without me," said the elephant bravely.

"We certainly won't," said Susan.

The elephant groaned. "I think there is smoke coming out of my ears, too. I can feel it."

Stephen and David folded back one of his big ears and tried to hold their grinning jack-o'-lanterns so they could see inside.

"I don't see any smoke," said Stephen.

David climbed right up the elephant's side and tried to push his lantern away inside the elephant's ear so he could see better.

"Don't you let *him* get in there," said the elephant nervously. He meant the lighted pumpkin head. "I don't want him burning his eyes inside me. Oh!"

"I think we should go on to Mrs. Jarvis's on the other side of the street," said Susan, "and then to Mrs. Craig's."

"I can't!" moaned the elephant. "I can't go any farther."

"Perhaps," said Susan carefully, "Mrs. Jarvis will have some licorice drops for us."

The elephant lifted his head and opened one

eye when Susan said that. "I'll try," he said weakly. Then, very slowly, as if he could hardly do it, he stood up again.

"Hurrah!" said David to his pumpkin lantern. "Hurrah! The elephant was on fire, but we put him out." He poked one finger right through the pumpkin's lighted nose.

"I've been waiting for you!" cried Mrs. Jarvis as the witch, the cat, the mouse, and the elephant all climbed up on the wide porch of her big white house. "I'm glad you've come. I was afraid the goblins might come and get me first. It *is* you, Susan, isn't it? And this must be you, Stephen," she said to the elephant. "My, you are getting to be a big boy!"

"I'm *me*," said the elephant, looking into the lighted hallway through the open front door. He was getting tired of everyone's thinking he was somebody else. "Look!" He took off his mask. "See? It's *me*."

"Of course," said Mrs. Jarvis, who was busy

putting things into the children's bags. "Of course. Now, let me see—"

Susan, who had disappeared behind Mrs. Jarvis for an instant, came running straight to the elephant. She held out both her hands to him. "See!" she cried. "Licorice drops! All for you!" It was a whole big bag full.

"Licorice drops!" shouted the elephant. "Licorice drops! Oh, thank you! Thank you, thank you!"

Soon they were all outside again. The moon was high now, and little white clouds were racing past it high in the dark sky. The will-o'-the-wisps slipped and whispered through the big trees in the dingle as they started for home, their jack-o'-lanterns bobbing. There was no one else moving on the wide old street of big old houses that ended in the tall black trees.

David was getting very sleepy. His lantern seemed twice as heavy as it had before. He was

3

"We could not possibly all go away even for this one night," said Mother gratefully to the elephant, "unless you were here to look after things."

"I'll take care of everything," the elephant promised.

"I'm leaving plenty of food in the refrigerator," she said, "and you can reach right through the pantry window to get it. The children are so anxious to see their cousins, and my sister is anxious to see us all. It seems a good time to drive to see them while their father is away on business again."

"I wish you could come with us," said Susan. She bent down to pat their spaniel, Jones.

"I have responsibilities here," said the elephant, importantly.

"Don't let Topsy eat Turvy," said David, talking about their two kittens, "and don't let Jones eat either of them, and don't you eat any of them. Don't eat anybody except tramps or that bad collie down the street."

"Nobody is going to eat anybody, David," said Susan laughing.

"Perhaps you can come next time," said Stephen, who knew the elephant was very sensitive. "Please don't go away while we are not here."

The elephant was very pleased. "I shall take

care of everything," he said once more with great dignity, just so they would not see how pleased he was.

As soon as they drove away late that afternoon, the elephant called a council at the barn. He stood inside, and the others stood just outside the big open doors.

"Fall in!" he ordered. He looked very dignified.

The elephant sometimes claimed he had been in the army, though he never said what army.

"Fall in what?" asked Turvy, the white kitten. He had been turning somersaults on the lawn and was a little dizzy.

"He means get into line," said Topsy, who had listened to some of the elephant's stories to Susan, Stephen, and David.

"Oh," said Jones. He had dirt on his nose

and muzzle for he had just been burying a bone down at the fence by the woods.

They all lined up before the elephant, who looked at them sternly.

"We shall guard this house tonight," he said, "in a military manner."

"What's that?" asked Turvy.

The elephant ignored him.

"Like soldiers," whispered Topsy.

Jones was listening so hard he began to pant, and there was dirt even on his tongue.

"As soon as it is dark," said the elephant, "we shall post our guards. Topsy, you will guard the side of the house toward the dingle. Turvy, you will guard the other side. Jones, you will be corporal of the guard covering all posts."

"Will I march back and forth?" asked Jones, trying not to scratch himself because he was afraid the elephant would not like it.

"Yes!"

"Will we carry guns?" asked Topsy, excited.

"Not exactly," said the elephant, frowning.

"He means not at all, I think," Turvy whispered.

"I shall be captain of the guard," said the elephant. "Jones, you will report to me at the barn."

"Yes, sir," said Jones.

The elephant looked them over coldly.

"Rations will be issued at six sharp," he said. "Dismissed."

"But when are we going to eat?" asked Turvy, who was always hungry.

"That's what he meant—at six o'clock," Topsy explained.

"Then why didn't he say so?"

"You never say exactly what you mean if you are grown up or important," Jones told them. "I don't know why."

"Dismissed!" roared the elephant again.

Topsy raced back to the lawn and began to flip-flop a new kind of somersault he had thought up while the elephant was talking. Turvy leaped up into a little dogwood tree on the lawn after a white butterfly which he never could catch. Jones just stayed where he was and scratched, grunting a little with satisfaction.

As soon as it was dark, the elephant marched his army of three to their posts, returned their salutes, and pretended to look at his wrist watch, though he did not have one.

"Report to me every hour, corporal," he ordered Jones, who was panting along after him. "An extra ration of one licorice drop to each man at nine o'clock."

The children's mother had left a big bag of licorice drops, which she knew the elephant was very fond of, for a special treat.

"Yes, sir," said Jones saluting. He tried not to wag his tail, for he thought the elephant might think that was improper.

Topsy, when they had left him alone, crept silently back and forth alongside the house. He was on the darkest side toward the woods. All he could see was the faint whiteness of the house and the black tops of trees and the sky with a few clouds rolling silently across it. A light wind was rustling the leaves in the trees.

"Eight o'clock and all's well," he kept muttering to himself. "Nine o'clock and all's well. Ten o'clock and all's well." He did not really know what time it was. He was just trying to see which number sounded best.

He wished he had a gun, but all he could find was a little straight maple branch. He put this over his shoulder and marched up and down. "Fifteen o'clock," he said, "and all's well."

Turvy did not know whether everything was well or not. He had never been out so late at night before. He wished he were under the kitchen stove where he liked to sleep, if he could not sneak into Susan's room and stay there undiscovered until it was too late for her to take him downstairs again. Besides he was very sleepy. He had turned so many somersaults he was not sure which way was right side up and which wrong way down. He decided he would ask Jones when he came by.

"Be on the alert," Jones whispered, coming up just then. "Orders from the elephant."

"Be on the what?" asked Turvy sleepily. He wet one paw and rubbed his eyes.

"Watch out for everything," said Jones, who was beginning to feel almost as important as the elephant.

Jones marched back to the barn.

"Pss't!" he whispered to the elephant.

"Pss't, what?" asked the elephant coldly.

"Pss't, *captain*," said Jones, who had forgotten for a moment.

"Yes?" asked the elephant impatiently. He was fussing with some papers he had found in an old school bag of Susan's, though it was too dark for him to see what was written on them.

"One car went by away down the street," reported Jones, "and an owl hooted once away off in the woods. One plane flew over. That is all."

"Back to your post," ordered the elephant. He returned Jones's salute and turned to his papers again.

As soon as Jones had gone, the elephant put down the papers and tiptoed to the door. He peered outside to make sure none of the others saw him coming and walked very quietly toward the house. When the elephant wanted to, he could move so silently that no one could hear him. He could slip through the woods without making any noise at all. Not a twig would crack. Leaves moved only as if touched gently by the wind.

Now he was like a gray ghost as he crept alongside the house to make sure the guards were on duty.

What he had forgotten was his shadow.

Topsy, walking back and forth with his make-believe gun on his shoulder and looking back every now and again to make sure he was not being followed, saw a huge shadow spreading slowly across the lawn that tipped down to the dingle. Dropping his gun he let out a frightened meow and raced as fast as he could around to the other side of the house.

He crashed right into Turvy who was creeping toward him. Both gave wild, frightened screeches. Jones, barking furiously, started for the spot, and ran headlong into the startled elephant who jumped high off the ground and came down trumpeting loudly.

Topsy, too frightened to know it was Turvy he had run into, was scratching and howling. Turvy broke and raced screaming right into Jones, who toppled over, jumped up, and ran off howling. The elephant scuttled for the barn.

"It was a ghost!" Topsy reported, out of

breath, his fur all ruffled. "He almost got me."

"There were no ghosts!" said the elephant who had just got into the barn himself. His heart was thumping.

"Thieves! Robbers!" cried Turvy. "They attacked me."

"I drove them off!" said Jones bravely. "They won't be back in a hurry."

"The house is safe," said the elephant. "I inspected it after they had fled. They won't be back."

Topsy, Turvy, and Jones crept trembling back into the darkness. They decided that no matter what the elephant said, they would stay close together. A pebble rattled loose in the driveway, and they all jumped. Topsy clutched Jones as a leaf fluttered down and fell right on him.

There was not a sound anywhere now except for the rustling of the leaves. It was warm and comfortable in the big barn. The elephant, who was glad the others had not found him out, felt that he was doing his job well. The house and everything in it would be safe until Susan, Stephen, David, and their mother returned. He began to feel a little sleepy. His head began to droop. He pulled it up sharply and looked once more at Susan's spelling papers, though he could not see what they were. His head drooped once more.

When Jones came back to report after he had made another tour of inspection, he found the elephant sound asleep. He did not know what to do. He ran off and got Topsy and Turvy. They could see better in the dark than Jones could.

"Yes," they told him. "He's sound asleep."

Before the others could stop him, Topsy just touched the tip of the elephant's trunk with his paw. They all leaped back as the elephant, who had been dreaming that he was leading an army into battle, jumped to his feet.

"Charge!" he shouted and rushed out.

Only he forgot which way the door was and knocked loose almost one whole side of the barn. Slowly he came back in again.

"Asleep!" he moaned. "I was asleep at my post. I forget whether you have to shoot me or hang me."

"We can't shoot you!" cried Topsy. "We don't have a gun."

"Yes," said the elephant thoughtfully. "That's true."

"And we have no rope strong enough to hang you," said Jones.

"Perhaps we could borrow one somewhere," suggested Turvy, who always wanted to be helpful.

"Silence!" roared the elephant.

"I think it would be better to shoot him,"

said Jones, "but even if we had a gun it would not be big enough to shoot an elephant."

"That's true also," said the elephant, hanging his head again. "I don't know what to do." He was terribly ashamed of himself.

"Perhaps," said Jones, who thought the elephant had been too hard on them all, "we could take you down to the river and drown you."

The elephant shivered.

"I have another idea," said Turvy, who was too sleepy now to care whether he felt right side up or upside down.

"Yes?" moaned the elephant.

"Weren't there some licorice drops left?"

"Quite a lot of them," said Jones licking his lips. Right then it did not seem to matter much what they did with the elephant if he could have another licorice drop.

"Then why don't we eat the rest of the licorice drops and then go to sleep. That would make everything all right.''

The elephant thought hard while they waited breathlessly.

"Yes," he decided finally, "I think that's the thing to do."

So they ate the rest of the licorice drops. Then they closed the door of the barn so that no one could get them and lay down and went to sleep.

Jones slept curled up in the crook of one of the elephant's knees. Turvy stretched himself out in a nice soft spot on the elephant's side. Topsy crawled under and covered himself up with one of the elephant's ears.

Just before they fell asleep, the elephant handed Turvy another licorice drop.

"I saved an extra one for you," he whispered. "Thank you."

4

It is nice to live in a barn, but it is nicer to live in a house. That is what the elephant thought that cold, dark, winter afternoon.

Mother, who was baking beans and rich, dark brown bread for their Saturday night dinner, had opened the kitchen door to let in some fresh air, and the elephant stood with his head stuck inside so that he could smell the delicious smells and watch David. David was lying on the kitchen floor shooting a toy gun at a small toy clown. If you shot the clown in the eye, his head popped straight up into the air.

Susan was in the living room changing her dolls' clothes. She had four dolls. One was a small doll named Ann; another was Dolly, the first doll she had ever had. Once Jones had got hold of Dolly and chewed off most of her hair and one ear, but it did not show much. The biggest doll was a bride with a veil and a long silk dress and even earrings. Her name was Julia. The last one was Agnes. She had only a plain cotton dress, so Susan, who liked Agnes best, was putting a fresh gingham apron on her and a hair ribbon to match.

When she had put them on, Susan picked up Agnes and hugged her. Then she hurried into the kitchen to show the elephant. "Doesn't she look nice now?" she asked him, holding Agnes up for him to see.

The elephant looked at Agnes coldly. "You know I don't like dolls," he told Susan.

"But you like Agnes. You know you do!"

"Not very much," said the elephant. He looked down at David. "Aim higher," he instructed, "and don't jerk the trigger. Just squeeze it."

David turned his gun around and aimed it right at the elephant. "I'll shoot *you*," he said. "Boom, boom, boom!"

"Now, David," exclaimed the children's mother quickly, "you know Father said you were not to aim your gun at people."

"The elephant's not people," said David.

"I'm better than people," said the elephant. "Let me try, now. It's my turn."

"No!" said David.

"It *is* his turn," said Susan, who had already forgiven the elephant because she knew he really liked Agnes even if he would not say so.

Mother opened the oven door. The beans

and brown bread smelled wonderful. "I wonder if I put in enough molasses," she said.

"I don't want any beans for supper!" cried David. "I'll just eat molasses, gallons and gallons of molasses!"

"Do you want me to taste them to see if they are all right?" asked the elephant eagerly. He pushed further into the room so that his trunk and head and part of his shoulders were inside. He filled the whole doorway.

David took careful aim and just squeezed the trigger, the way the elephant had told him. The clown's head flew straight into the air, bounced on the ceiling, and clattered to the floor.

They were all so startled that Mother jumped back from the stove, and Susan dropped Agnes. The elephant jerked in the doorway and banged his head.

"I did it! I did it! I did it!" shouted David. "I shot the clown right in the eye!"

"Don't cry," Susan whispered to Agnes.

"Don't cry." She hugged the doll hard and straightened out her hair ribbon.

The elephant did not say anything. He just rolled his eyes toward one side of the door and then the other and looked a little funny.

David was trying to jam the clown's head back on so he could shoot it off again.

"Oh!" said Mother, looking at the old clock which ticked on the kitchen wall. "It's later than I thought. I must hurry to the station to get Father, and Stephen will be coming home from the Cub Scouts, and they'll be as hungry as bears! Susan, will you get my hat and coat, please, and my bag? Now, where did I put the keys to the car?"

"Yes, Mother," said Susan, hurrying off.

"Can I go with you?" asked David. "Can I go? I want to go with you."

"I think my rubbers are on the porch," Mother said to the elephant. She stepped close to him and smiled as she waited for him to get out of her way.

The elephant looked back at Mother, but he did not move, and Mother looked surprised. "My rubbers," she explained. "They're just—"

"I can't move," said the elephant. "I'm stuck. I'm stuck in the doorway."

"My goodness!" gasped Mother.

"Hurrah!" cried David.

"You can't be!" exclaimed Susan, who had come back with her mother's coat and bag.

"I don't want to come now, Mother!" said David. "I just want to stay here and watch the elephant be stuck in the doorway."

"I don't want to be stuck in the doorway!" said the elephant unhappily.

"Now, don't you worry," said Susan, patting his trunk. "Everything will be all right."

"Oh!" exclaimed Mother. "I'll be late. I'll go out the front door. I'm sorry," she told the elephant, "but I promised Father I'd meet his train."

The elephant was perspiring now. Drops of perspiration stood out on his forehead. He wriggled as hard as he could, but he could not budge.

"Try sucking in your breath," said Susan. "Hold it as long as you can and try to back out."

The elephant sucked in more breath than he usually sucked in, and he pushed hard against the floor with his front feet, but it was no use. He stuck harder than ever.

"I know! I know!" cried David. "I'll shoot him in the eye. Then his head will come off, and he can get right through."

"I don't want my head to come off!" roared the elephant. "I just want to get loose."

"We could put your head back on again," argued David.

"Now stop being silly," ordered Susan. "Try

pushing all your breath out," she told the elephant.

The elephant tried until his eyes bulged, and he actually did move just a little bit, but when he had to breathe again he was locked more tightly into the doorway than ever before.

"Oh, dear!" sighed Susan.

"Both of you push," said the elephant, "and I'll try, too."

"What's the matter?" called someone from the outside. "What's happened?" It was Stephen.

"The elephant's stuck! The elephant's stuck! The elephant's stuck!" sang David.

Stephen came crawling through between the elephant's legs. He had on his Cub Scout uniform and a big, thick Hudson's Bay parka. It was white with stripes like peppermint candy. As soon as he was inside, he stood up and looked at the elephant.

"We must figure this out," he said. Stephen was very thoughtful.

He looked carefully at the sides of the door, at the floor, and at the elephant. Then he crawled through again and looked at the elephant from the outside. Then he came in again and stood up and looked into the elephant's face. "H'm," he said thoughtfully, just the way the Cub Scoutmaster said it.

"Don't stand there saying 'H'm!' " roared the elephant. "Are you going to keep me stuck here until I roast inside and freeze outside? You just want to keep me here while you eat all the baked beans and brown bread!"

"First," said Stephen, trying hard to remember all the things he had read in school, "I have to get a crowbar and a rope and an axe from the cellar. Don't you go away until I come back."

"How can he?" asked David.

"David, be still," said Susan gently. She

wiped the elephant's face with her handkerchief. "Father will be here right away. He can fix it."

"Don't you stick me with that thing!" shouted the elephant, as Stephen came back with the crowbar. "Don't you dare stick me with that! What are you going to do with the rope?"

"I don't know," said Stephen. Then he remembered what it was that he had read. "We'll build a fire under him," he said to Susan. "Then he'll just leap through. It's what they used to do with balky mules and horses."

"No!" cried the elephant. Then he cried even louder. "Oh! Oh!"

David had got a bar of soap and a hammer, and he was trying to drive the soap down between the elephant and one side of the doorway to make it slippery. He had hit the elephant instead.

"Here, here now, what's all this?" asked Father cheerfully. They were so excited they had not heard the car come back. "H'm," he said, just the way Stephen had said it. "M'm. These little problems can always be solved." Father worked for the government and was used to fixing things.

"They're trying to kill me," said the elephant piteously.

"Oh, I'm sure they are not trying to do that," said Father quietly. "Try not to upset yourself. Stephen, let me see that crowbar. Perhaps I can pry loose this upright. David, run down and get the can of grease off my work bench. Your soap idea is not so bad after all. Susan, you just stay out of the way."

The crowbar just splintered some of the wood away from the side of the door. It did not help except to put a few splinters into the elephant. Then Father made a big belt of grease across the elephant's back and as far down his sides as he could reach.

"Now, all together, everyone!" he called. David and Stephen and Susan and Mother and Father all leaned against the elephant's chest and pushed as hard as they could.

The doorway bulged and creaked, but the elephant could not move at all. It was no use.

"Don't cry," Susan whispered to the elephant. "Don't cry."

"I wasn't going to," said the elephant, but a tear trickled out of one eye. Susan wiped it away before anyone else could see.

"If you were stuck in a doorway," the elephant said very severely to Father, "I'd get you out. I can't breathe. I'm beginning to suffocate. You scraped my sides."

Father studied him for a moment. He looked at the elephant in front. He looked at as much of his sides as he could see. He crawled under him, as Stephen had done, and looked at him from the back. "Bring me a tape measure, some-one," he called.

"What are you going to do?" demanded the elephant, as Susan got the tape measure out of the drawer of the sewing machine and pushed it under him to Father. The elephant tried and tried to look around, the doorway creaking and the kitchen wall quivering as he strained to see. He could not see behind him at all, and it made him feel worse than ever. Stephen was out there too, and he and Father were whispering. "What are you going to do?"

Father crawled back into the kitchen, dragging the tape measure after him.

"I'll have you out of there in a minute," he said triumphantly. "Mother, please come into the living room."

"I knew Father would fix it," Susan said gently to the elephant.

"Why won't anyone let me shoot him in the eye so his head will come off?" pleaded David. He pointed his gun again.

"No! No! No!" The elephant squeezed his eyes tight shut.

Father began to crawl out under him again. Halfway out he stopped. "This may hurt a little just for a second," he said, looking up from under the elephant's stomach, "but it will be over before you know what is happening, and you'll be free."

"No! No!" cried the elephant again, even though he did not know what Father was planning to do. He did not see the big pin hidden in Father's hand.

"Steady now!" shouted Father from outside. "Hold very still."

"Steady!" cried Stephen.

"Ow!" screamed the elephant.

He lunged through the doorway with all his might. The wood cracked loudly, and another long piece splintered off. The big calendar fell off the wall. Mother and Susan jumped back out of the way. "Ow!" cried the elephant again as he banged his head on the ceiling and burned his foot on the oven. "Ow!"

"I didn't mean to hurt you," said Father, coming in and patting the elephant hard, "but I knew we could do it. You're all right now."

Stephen was smiling all over. He and David were squeezed against the wall because the elephant took up almost the whole kitchen. Mother and Susan stood in the big doorway into the living room.

"Didn't I tell you it would work?" bragged Father. "Just a mild sting for a second, and the job was done."

Stephen was still smiling as if he had done it all by himself. The elephant looked at him unpleasantly.

"Yes," said Mother, "but—"

"We're all as hungry as can be," said Father,

who thought the elephant would feel better after he had had something to eat. "Those beans and brown bread smell awfully good."

"Of course," said Mother, and Susan ran to help her set upright the kitchen table, which had been knocked over. "Of course, but don't you see? The elephant's inside, now. How are you going to get him out again?"

"Oh!" said Father, who had never thought of that.

"Oh!" said Stephen, who had not thought of it either.

"That's fine," said the elephant, who had known it all along. "I'll just stay here, and they can live in the barn."

"I'll shoot him!" shouted David. "I'll shoot him. I don't want Father to sleep in the barn. Stephen can sleep there if he wants to. He's a Cub Scout."

"I could use my new sleeping bag," said Stephen.

Susan said nothing. She got the elephant a big plate of steaming baked beans and a thick slice of the spicy brown bread and put them on the kitchen table for him.

"Thank you," said the elephant, and he and Susan both took a bite of the brown bread. The elephant ignored Father.

"What are we going to do now?" demanded Father. He acted as if it were all David's fault or the elephant's or Susan's or Mother's.

"I could stick *you* with a pin," said the elephant, "and see how *you'd* like it."

"We shall all eat our dinner and decide after that what to do," said Mother firmly. "Everything is all ready in the dining room. More beans?" she asked the elephant.

"Yes, please," said the elephant, "and some more brown bread, please, and a little more chili sauce for my beans." He did not even look at Father as he added, "Perhaps we had better knock the wall out of this side of the house or

I could lift up the roof over the kitchen."

"No!" cried Father.

The elephant just smiled as he ate and ate and ate.

The others went into the dining room for their dinner, but Father was too worried. "What do you think I should do?" he asked the elephant.

The elephant took another spoonful of beans. "You could burn down the house," he said.

"You know I can't do that!" Father looked at the elephant carefully. "Perhaps if you did not eat anything for a week you'd be thin enough to get back through."

The elephant ate the rest of his brown bread before he answered. "I'm afraid I'll just have to knock down the side of the house, as I said first. You can get it built up again."

"In the middle of winter? We'd freeze!"

"You might," said the elephant. "It still hurts where you stuck me with that pin."

"I had to stick you and I had to stick you from the back. You would not have let me stick you in front."

"I think I would feel better," said the elephant, moving toward Father a little, "if you'd let me stick you with a pin."

"No!" said Father. He backed into the dining room.

"He doesn't mean it," said Susan quickly. "You know he doesn't mean it. You shouldn't tease Father that way," she said to the elephant.

"Where's that gun?" asked the elephant loudly. "I might want to shoot David."

"Good!" called David from the dining room. He came running out, grabbed his gun from the floor and handed it to the elephant. "Shoot me. I want to see if my head will come off. Please, shoot me!"

"David, come back and finish your dinner," his mother called. She made Father come, too.

"Everything will be all right," the elephant told Susan quietly. "I know what to do." Then he raised his voice. "Susan, will you hand me that crowbar, please. I'll start taking down the doorway."

Father charged out of the dining room with his napkin in his hand.

The elephant just handed him the crowbar, walked through the wide doors into the living room, opened the other half of the double front door of the house, which was seldom used, and stepped outside.

Father just watched. He was too surprised to speak.

Outside, the elephant turned and bowed. "Good night," he said to Father very stiffly. "Good night," he said to the others, who had

all crowded behind Father. "I think I shall go to bed now. Thank you for my dinner."

Susan slipped out into the darkness and the cold. "I knew you would know what to do," she whispered.

"Of course," said the elephant proudly.

"Does it still hurt?"

"It certainly does." The elephant was very dignified.

Susan slipped Agnes out of her arms. "Would you like to keep her for company tonight?"

"Yes, I would," whispered the elephant. "Thank you very much." He took Agnes carefully from Susan so as not to muss the apron and the hair ribbon, and the elephant, with the doll, trudged slowly up the drive to the barn just as the moon was coming up over the trees down toward the frozen river.

5

Halfway up the hill on which he was pulling Susan, Stephen, and David on their sleds, the elephant stopped.

"I won't go one step farther," he said. He was very angry.

"Giddap!" shouted David. "Giddap!" His sled was the last, tied behind Stephen's, which was tied behind Susan's.

The elephant did not answer. He just stood there looking stubborn.

"Please pull us the rest of the way up!" begged Susan.

"We let you ride down every time," said Stephen. "It's only fair if you pull us back up."

"I don't like to ride just downhill," said the elephant. "I like to ride uphill, too."

"Giddap!" cried David. "Giddap! Oh!"

He bounced up and down so hard on his sled

that all of a sudden he fell off and twisted around and around and slid all the way to the bottom of the hill without his sled.

Susan and Stephen laughed and laughed, but the elephant would not even turn around to look.

"I think you should pull me up the hill," he said. "I've been pulling you up all afternoon."

"You know we can't do that," said Stephen. "You're too big. Besides you know you hardly feel it when you pull us up. You said so yourself."

"That doesn't make it fair," said the elephant. He still would not look at them but just stood there. "London *was* the center of the world when I was there. I don't care what your father says."

"I do wish you and Father would not argue so," said Susan.

"Father has been in London lots of times,"

said Stephen. "The government sends him."

"I've been there more," said the elephant. "I was there even before London was there."

"You know you weren't," scolded Susan. "Father doesn't like it when you say things like that."

"Well, I feel as if I had been," said the elephant, turning now to look at Susan. "That's what I meant when I said London was the center of the world when I was there. Where I am is always the center of the world because that's the way it feels."

"But that isn't what you said when you and Father were talking," said Stephen.

"He should have known it anyway," said the elephant coldly. "I knew what he meant."

"Father—" Susan began.

Stephen interrupted her. He was tired of sitting still. "If you don't pull us up, I don't think we should let you slide down on our sleds," he said to the elephant.

"I can slide down on myself without any sled at all," the elephant answered. "See?"

He turned around, sat down, and slid down the hill so fast he almost could not stop when he came to the fence by the woods below the house. He had to use his feet for brakes and stopped in a cloud of snow.

Susan and Stephen twisted their sleds around in a second. They came flying into the snow cloud the elephant had made. David, who had clambered uphill, came three seconds later, but he fell off before he reached the others.

"Do it again!" David cried to the elephant. He wriggled to get the snow out of his sleeves. His jacket was red and his cap was red and his nose was redder still. "I'm going to slide down without my sled, too!"

David ran up to the top of the hill and came down the same way the elephant had come, only he was so much smaller he did not toss up the cloud of snow. Instead he disappeared right into a snow drift that was almost over his head. The others had to pull him out and brush him off.

"Come on!" cried the elephant.

Forgetting all about wanting them to pull him up the hill and all about his argument with Father at breakfast, he galloped up to the top. Susan and Stephen and David ran after him, and then came spinning down the hill again, Susan and Stephen sliding on their sleds, the elephant and David just sliding on themselves.

This time all the others landed on the elephant. He was upside down in the soft snow and waving his legs in the air as they bounced on his stomach.

"Oof!" cried the elephant as Stephen landed on him. "Oomph!" he said when Susan landed a second later. "Hssst!" he said when David struck. It sounded as if the air were coming out of a bicycle pump.

David had so much snow on him he looked like a little walking snowman.

That gave Stephen an idea. "Let's make a snowman!"

"Let's!" echoed Susan, "only—"

"Only what?" asked the elephant as he came sliding down one more time.

"Let's make a great big snow elephant instead."

"Yes!" shouted David, "a great, great, great big snow elephant!" He threw out his arms so hard to show how big an elephant he meant that he fell right over into the snow once more.

"I don't know," said the elephant slowly, as he picked up David and shook him a little to get some of the snow off. "I'm cold. I want to go inside."

He was not really cold, and he did not want to go in, but he was not sure he knew how to make a snow elephant.

"I know what we could do," said Stephen. "You could sit down here at the bottom of the hill, and we could put snow all over you. Then we would have a snow elephant."

"No," said the elephant.

"Please!" begged Susan.

"No!" said the elephant.

"We'll get Mother to give you extra cocoa and three extra oatmeal cookies," Stephen promised.

"I'm tired of cocoa and cookies," said the elephant. "I want tea with ginger in it and toast with cheese melted on it."

"Mother will make that for us," said Susan quickly.

"Lots of tea with big pieces of preserved ginger? So much melted cheese it drips all over and you can hardly see the toast?" asked the elephant, his mouth watering.

"Yes!"

"All right then!"

With a few whisks of his trunk, the elephant scooped up a great heap of snow. He piled even more on top of that. Soon he had made a whole little hill of snow. Then he sat down right in the middle of it.

The children had run for shovels, and Stephen had got the stepladder. They began to cover the elephant with snow, packing it hard against him.

"Ooo! It's cold!" complained the elephant. "Ooo! I'm turning to ice!" He shivered and some of the snow fell off.

"Sit still!" shouted Stephen, who was up on the ladder putting shovelfuls of snow on the elephant's head while Susan and David were covering his sides.

The elephant sat still, thinking of steaming hot tea and hot preserved ginger and warm, melting cheese. Soon they had every bit of him covered except his eyes and his trunk. The elephant blinked at them from inside the snow, and his voice was muffled as if he were far away. The children stood back and looked at him in awe.

"The elephant is the biggest snowman in the world," said David.

"You're *beautiful!*" said Susan. "I'm going to get Mother to come and look." She ran toward the house.

"I'm coming out," said the elephant suddenly. "It's lonesome in here, and it's dark. Besides, I want to see myself."

"No," said Stephen. "The snow will fall down."

"I'm coming out," said the elephant. "I don't want to be an elephant inside an elephant."

"Come out!" cried David. "Then I'll go inside, and I'll be the elephant."

"I'm the elephant," said the elephant. "You can't be me, but I have to come out. If I stay in here I might freeze."

So Stephen and David shoveled away some of the snow in back, and the elephant made himself as small as he could and slipped out very carefully so that none of the great snow elephant broke off. Then they all stood back and looked at the snow elephant.

The elephant frowned, and there was snow in the creases the frown made in his forehead. "He is not as good looking as I am," he said. "I am much better looking than he is."

"Now I'll be the elephant!" shouted David. He hurried around to the back of the snow elephant and got inside.

Stephen went inside, too, and they pulled the stepladder in after them.

Soon David, standing on the very top of the ladder, was looking out through the eye holes. Stephen put his right arm through the hole for the elephant's trunk and waved it around. As he was wearing his Hudson's Bay parka and

bright green mittens, his arm and hand made a funny-looking trunk.

"I'm an elephant! I'm really an elephant now!" shouted David from the inside. His voice sounded hollow and funny. "Look at me! I'm an elephant!"

The elephant frowned even harder. He did not like this snow elephant, which was exactly as large as he was, or David's eyes looking out where his should be or Stephen's arm waggling like his trunk.

He thought Stephen and David were making fun of him. He did not want to play any more. He did not even want his tea and ginger and melted cheese on toast. Slowly he turned and walked away. He went around the far side of the house where he would not have to look at the snow elephant.

"Look, Mother!" cried Susan a few minutes later. "Look at the elephant all covered with snow."

Stephen had pulled his arm back through, so their mother did not know it was really David and Stephen inside the snow elephant.

"Why," she said to the snow elephant, "the children have completely covered you! Aren't you cold? I think you have all been playing in the snow long enough. You had all better come and get dry and warm. I'll get the tea and cheese ready."

"I think we ought to stay out a little longer," said David from inside the snow elephant. He blinked at his mother, but she thought it was the real elephant blinking.

"You sound just like David! You are very good to take care of them so well and play with them like this, but I don't want you to catch cold either, you know."

"He's a wonderful elephant," said Susan, who thought the elephant was still inside.

Inside, Stephen was both trying hard not to laugh himself and to keep David from telling their mother it was they. "S'sh!" he whispered, holding David tightly so that he would not fall off the ladder.

"What did you say?" Susan asked, but they held their breaths and did not answer.

"I must get back to the house," said Mother. "Susan, you come and help me, please."

"Good-bye," Susan said to what she still thought was the real elephant. "You'll come right away, won't you? Bring the boys, too. Where are they?"

As soon as Susan and their mother had gone, Stephen and David crawled out through the back of the snow elephant. They laughed until they were rolling around in the snow to think how they had fooled Mother and Susan. Then Stephen took the step ladder back to the barn. In a minute he was back. The elephant, who had seen and heard it all as he peeked around a corner of the house, came back, too.

He felt very unhappy. He was jealous of this

snow elephant. He wanted to be the only elephant who lived with Susan and Stephen and David.

"We have to go inside now," said Stephen. "We'll get the tea and the cheese and toast and bring them to the barn as soon as they are ready."

"Let's have just one more slide," suggested the elephant eagerly.

"Let's!" cried David.

"Well," said Stephen, "I suppose we can have just one more!"

The elephant raced to the top of the hill, the boys after him with their sleds.

"Now!" cried the elephant, throwing himself forward on his stomach with his front legs stretched away out.

With the boys right after him on their sleds, he coasted down the hill as fast as he could go. The snow was getting very slippery now that the sun was beginning to go down. They went very fast.

This time the elephant did not even try to stop. With the boys right after him, he crashed head-on into the snow elephant, and it came toppling down all over them.

The elephant got his head out of the snow first, and he just sat there smiling widely. "No more snow elephant!" he said. He was not angry or jealous any more.

"It was fun building him and it was fun knocking him down," said Stephen, as soon as he had got some of the snow out of his mouth and eyes and ears.

The top of David's cap came up first, then the rest of him. "No more snow elephant!" he shouted. He pounded the elephant happily. "You're the only elephant we have again."

"That's right," said the elephant, who was even more happy about it than David. "I'm the only one." He sniffed. Then he sniffed again. "Tea—ginger." He sniffed a third time. "Cheese melting!"

They all jumped up and ran toward the house.

6

"You," said the elephant to the lifeguard, who was sitting on his tower watching the people in the water and along the wide beach of white sand, "can save only one drowning person at a time. I can save twenty or thirty people all at once if I want to. I just let them climb on my back, and then I swim in."

Now that school was closed, Stephen, Susan, David and the elephant were at the seaside having a wonderful time. That morning the children's mother and father had driven them from the cottage down to the water to stay all day. They were going to come back for them in the afternoon. Mother knew that the elephant would take care of the others.

The lifeguard, who had big shoulders and lots of sunburned muscles, was very angry. As he sat on top of his wooden tower on a low stool under his red and white striped umbrella and as the elephant was standing on the sand, one was just about as tall as the other. They looked closely into each other's eyes.

"You can't either save more people than I can," said the lifeguard angrily.

"All right," said the elephant. "Just start drowning a few and I'll show you."

"I can't do that!"

"You're afraid," said the elephant.

"I am not!" cried the lifeguard.

"Then *I'll* drown a few," said the elephant. "Not all the way, of course, but just a little bit. Then I'll save them. Watch me." He started toward the bright blue water which was splashing in with a great roar along the beach.

"Come back!" ordered Susan. "You know you don't mean it," she scolded the elephant. "You wouldn't really drown anybody ever!"

"I might drown *him*," said the elephant, looking at the lifeguard again. "Probably I'll drown him and not even save him afterward."

The lifeguard grew angrier than ever.

"Anyway," he said to the elephant, "I can dive better than you."

"No, you can't," said the elephant. "I can dive better than anybody."

"Can you do a double back flip off the high board out there on the float?"

"I can do a *double* double back flip and a

jackknife at the same time," boasted the elephant.

"Let's see you do it," said the guard scornfully.

The elephant shook his head.

"If I dived off the high board in a double double back flip with a jackknife, it would make such a big splash all the people would pop out of the water."

"You can't do it!"

"And it would make such a big wave it would upset all the ships everywhere and a great big tide would wash up everywhere—even in Russia."

Stephen, who had been trying to stand on his head in the sand and not paying much attention, heard him. He stood on his feet. "Most of Russia isn't on the ocean," said Stephen, who had read about Russia in school.

101

"That just makes it worse," said the elephant, who didn't really know where Russia is. "If a big wave came up there and washed everything away and Russia isn't even *on* the ocean, it would be worse than if it were."

"Yes, of course," said Susan quickly, just to keep the elephant quiet. "Come on," she urged him. "Let's all go into the water again."

David, who had been chasing a big horseshoe crab, followed it right into the water. He went in too far, and a whitecap that was taller than he was took him and spun him around and upside down like a pinwheel.

The lifeguard jumped down from his tower, ran across the sand, and snatched David out of the water. He turned him upside down so that the water would spill out of him.

David choked and sputtered.

"Let me go! Let me go!" he cried, as soon as he could talk at all. Upside down, he began to pound the lifeguard on his sunburned knees. "I don't want you to save me, you! I want the elephant to save me!"

As soon as he was upright again, David broke away from the lifeguard and dashed back into the water. Another wave grabbed him and swirled him upside down and almost inside out.

Without seeming even to look around, the elephant whipped out his trunk and hoisted David back to dry land. He held him upside down, too, for a minute and shook him a little so that salt spray flashed off David in diamond-bright drops.

"See?" said the elephant coldly to the lifeguard.

"See?" choked David, pulling a small clam out of his hair.

"I should put you off the beach," the lifeguard told the elephant. "See that sign? It says 'No Dogs Allowed.' "

"The elephant isn't a dog," said Stephen indignantly.

"I'll make the elephant step on you," David told the lifeguard. "You'll go so deep in the sand, no one will ever find you."

"The elephant would never do that, either," said Susan quickly.

"He'd do it to me if he could," said the elephant, watching the lifeguard closely.

"Let's all go back into the water," Susan urged again.

A few drops of water had showered over the lifeguard as the elephant shook out David. Some had not yet dried on his face. Suddenly David saw them. He shouted and pointed at him.

"The lifeguard's crying!" he shouted. "He's a crybaby! He's a scaredy-cat!"

Then he ran as fast as he could, and the others all ran after him.

Stephen, Susan, David, and the elephant raced

far up the beach, away from the people who were in swimming or lying on the sand. They raced so far that the lifeguard's tower with its red and white umbrella was only a bright little speck in the distance.

No one else was around where the white waves curled into a little cove and lapped over the white sand. There was a beautiful pool of clear, blue water warmed by the bright sun. They splashed into the water and Stephen dived off the elephant's back and swam under his stomach. Susan, in her pretty white bathing suit, paddled around them with a sidestroke, while David just stood in the water up to his knees and tried to splash the others.

Then the elephant put them all on his back and swam around and around while the others shouted happily. It was like being on a merry-go-round.

Then the elephant played submarine. He

walked around and around on the bottom with just the tip of his trunk sticking out of the water like a conning tower so that he could breathe. Stephen dived some more and swam under water. Susan held David under his stomach so that he could swim safely in the shallow water.

When they were all so tired they could not swim any more, they came out of the water and played in the sand. They collected hundreds of pretty shells. They dug in the sand and made forts and castles. They found big clams and oddly shaped bits of wood washed up by the tides, and then they watched a line of fat porpoises swimming and playing far out in the water.

After a while Stephen and Susan went back to where they had hidden the big lunch basket and the thermos jug full of lemonade. Susan spread out the tablecloth on the sand and they ate and ate and ate—cream cheese and ginger sandwiches with cool lettuce in them and bananas and date bread sandwiches and cookies and cake and more sandwiches and more cake. They drank lemonade and ate until they were all so full and so happy that they could no longer stay awake.

The elephant sighed and stretched himself out in the sand. Susan and Stephen sighed and snuggled down against him in his shade. Little David rubbed his stomach and his eyes and fell asleep almost while he was standing there. Susan pulled the old plaid beach blanket their father had once brought them from Canada over the three of them so they would not get too sunburned, and they all dozed off.

The sun was gently warm. A little breeze swung in from the sea. The air smelled of salt water and the pine woods inshore and the clumps of drying seaweed and beach flowers on the white sand dunes behind them. The lapping sound of the water with the unending dull roar of the breakers down the beach lulled them.

How long they slept they did not know. The sun was starting down a little and the sea was not quite so bright. Stephen said he could not tell the time by the sun because the tall pines behind them were throwing too much shadow now.

"Perhaps we should go," said Susan sleepily. "Mother and Father will soon be coming for us."

"Yes, I think we should go," said the elephant, but he did not open his eyes.

Stephen just sat looking at the white sails of some small boats scudding through the water so far out that they were almost out of sight.

David had not yet waked. When he did, a few minutes later, he kicked off the blanket, scrambled to his feet, and raced back down the beach. Susan and Stephen snatched up the lunch basket and the plaid robe and ran after him. For a moment, the elephant did not move. Then he pushed himself up and galloped so fast that he soon caught up to them.

It was almost high tide now. The long, white beach was much narrower than when they had raced along it before. As they drew nearer to the place they had been that morning, they saw that only a few people were at the shore now and only a few cars in the parking lot. What the elephant saw was that the lifeguard had gone too and that his tower was empty.

He put on more speed and thundered past Susan, Stephen, and David. As soon as he got there, he climbed right up into the tower and sat on the lifeguard's stool.

He picked up the lifeguard's megaphone and shouted back at the children.

"Ahoy, there!" he shouted. "Ahoy there!"

"The elephant's the lifeguard now!" cried David gleefully. "The elephant's the lifeguard!"

The elephant pretended not to notice them

as, all out of breath, Susan, Stephen, and David reached the foot of his tower. Because the tide was coming in, the tower was only a few feet from the water now.

The elephant pulled a big white towel across his shoulders, just the way the lifeguard did. He picked up the lifeguard's binoculars and carefully looked out over the water. He looked carefully at everybody who was in the water and then away out to sea. Then he looked down at Susan, Stephen, and David.

They laughed up at him. Then Susan and Stephen decided they would get wet just once more. The elephant let them get a little way down the beach. Then he took the lifeguard's whistle off its hook and blew it sharply. Very importantly he waved them back.

"That's all for today," he announced.

"Just once more," begged Stephen.

"Too dangerous," said the elephant, just as if he were really the lifeguard.

"I want to go back into the water, too," said David, straining his neck to look up at him.

The elephant pretended he did not hear. He stood up and stretched himself. He felt all his muscles.

Laughing, Susan and Stephen had come back, but the elephant did not look at them. He grabbed up the binoculars once more and looked away out to sea. Then he snatched up his megaphone as if he were going to shout at someone.

"Ahoy, there!" he roared. "Ahoy, there!"

They all looked out to see whom he was calling.

"Ahoy, there!" roared the elephant again. While they watched him, he put down his binoculars and megaphone and turned his head sidewise a little as if he were listening. After a moment, he smiled and nodded. He listened some more and nodded and smiled again.

"Whom are you talking to?" asked Susan.

The elephant looked down at her as if he were surprised. "One of my friends across the ocean, of course," he explained.

"What's he saying?" asked Stephen.

"He says," said the elephant, "that I am a lot better lifeguard than that fellow who was here this morning. He says I'm the best lifeguard there is!"

"You know you can't call clear across the ocean," said Susan.

"Is he another elephant?" asked David.

"How do you know he said that?" Stephen wanted to know.

"Thank you!" roared the elephant back across the wide ocean. "I hope you are well. Yes, it's wonderful here!"

He took the big red and white umbrella out of its socket and began to wave it as if he were signaling to someone the others could not see. It was then that he lost his balance. He fell against the wooden railing around the top of the tower, and it broke like a matchstick.

With a tremendous splash, the elephant fell right into the water.

"Oof!" he said.

Part of him was on the sand, but most of him was in the waves all tangled up with the red and white umbrella, the little megaphone, and the parts of the tower that had broken off.

Quickly, Susan and Stephen jumped in and began to tug at his ears to drag him to safety. David grabbed the elephant's tail and pulled as hard as he could.

The elephant, swooshing salt water out of his trunk and shaking it out of his eyes, got to his knees. Slowly he got to his feet and backed thoughtfully out of the water. He spat out the lifeguard's whistle, which he had almost swallowed.

"Thank you! Thank you!" he said chokingly

to Stephen and Susan and David.

"We saved the elephant!" cried David. "We saved the elephant!"

"Of course you did," said the elephant. "Thank you very much." Stephen was busy putting back the lifeguard's umbrella and binoculars and megaphone. The elephant winked at Susan as, limping a little, he started to walk across the sand.

"The elephant's the best lifeguard in the world!" David shouted to the ocean and the sky. "He's the best in the whole world, and we saved him!"